Kelly Fernández

An Imprint of
SCHOLASTIC

Library of Congress Control Number: 2020946443

ISBN 978-1-338-26419-7 (hardcover)
ISBN 978-1-338-26418-0 (paperback)

10 9 8 7 6 5 4 3 2   21 22 23 24 25

Printed in China   62
First edition, October 2021

Edited by Cassandra Pelham Fulton
Book design by Kelly Fernández and Steve Ponzo
Creative Director: Phil Falco
Publisher: David Saylor

TO ANYONE LOST
IN A DEEP, DARK CAVE

1
THE BIG
MANGO MESS

4

5

11

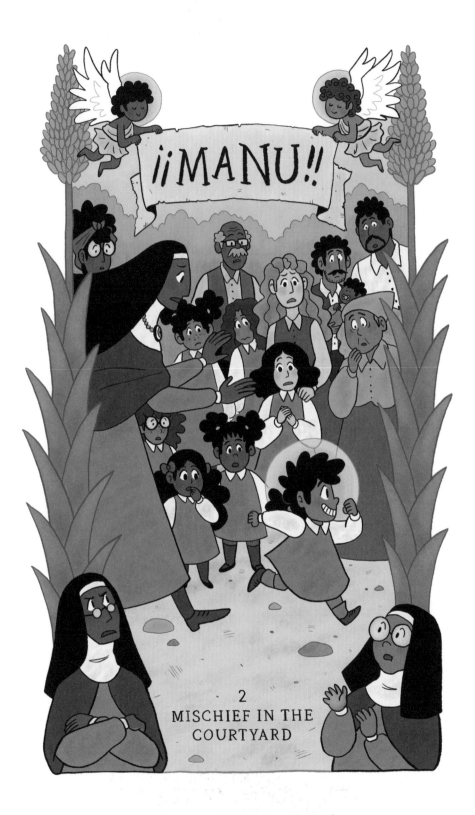

¡¡MANU!!

2
MISCHIEF IN THE
COURTYARD

28

31

34

40

51

59

UGH! THERE'S ALWAYS A CATCH!

CURSES AND CURES

My! You smell wonderful.

sniff sniff

If you forgot to apply your potion this morning, I can send you to Sister Noela's office.

Nah! I don't need it anymore!

GLOW

BAM

Uh-oh...it's not stopping!

112

113

135

CHATTER
CHATTER
CHATTER

Hmph!

I was planning to tell her everything when she was much older.

But now I realize that she needed to know sooner. Maybe she wouldn't have done all this if she knew where she came from...

And could explore that part of herself.

SCREEEEE

?!

HURRY! PERFORM THE EXORCISM!

Right!

7
CATCHING
UP

The End

AUTHOR'S NOTE

While writing this book, I reflected on my childhood and the stories my family would tell about curses, ghosts, monsters, and brujas. It was easy to see how brujería (the Spanish word for witchcraft) was ingrained in our daily lives as Dominicans, including the way we seamlessly wove it into our Roman Catholic traditions. Though we aren't witches ourselves, we heed and respect many of these beliefs and rituals that have taken root in our culture.

From what I've learned through research and speaking to my Latinx friends and colleagues, brujería varies from country to country, culture to culture, and family to family. My personal experiences involved wearing both our mal de ojo bracelets and prayer rosaries as protection from danger and bad intentions, singing the "colita de rana" chant whenever someone hurt themselves, and reciting "Our Father" and "Hail Mary" at bedtime. My newborn cousins never went without spit and thread on their foreheads (for warding off hiccups), and were also baptized in church.

This book is my way of exploring and celebrating the parts of myself that are still mysterious to me. Though both sides of my family immigrated to the United States from the Dominican Republic, there are still things I'm learning about my history, culture, and language every day. I hope *Manu* inspires you not to hide or reject the mysterious parts of yourself, but to embrace and learn more about them.

Kelly

Sketchbook

Here are some drawings and cartoons
that I made while developing Manu!

ACKNOWLEDGMENTS

Thank you to my family for being my first fans, editors, and collaborators. To Cassandra, David, María, Phil, Steve, Emily, Holland, and everyone at Scholastic who believed in me and helped make this book a reality — I can never thank you all enough! You've made the dreams I've had since I was ten years old come true.

Thank you to my agent, Tanya, for all your advice, cheerleading, and brainstorming over the phone. To Andrés, Na, Mei Lan, and Pablo, for being the second family I didn't know I needed. To my colleagues at FPPL for all the love you've shown me and for your acceptance. Big hugs and thanks to Kat, Steph, and Lucía for being there when I was at my lowest points. And to everyone who has supported my work online and in person throughout the years. I wouldn't be here without your encouragement!

Last but not least: Thank you, Angelica, for your invaluable assistance, feedback, and love. You're my partner in crime, and I feel incredibly lucky to have you in my life. Whenever you're with me, I feel like a million pesos!

KELLY FERNÁNDEZ makes comics that are inspired by her daily experiences, Dominican heritage, and American culture. Her work has been featured in comics anthologies, and she won a Chicago Alternative Comics Expo Cupcake Award for her minicomic *Cuidando*. Kelly is a winner of the Get Published by Graphix contest, and *Manu* is her debut graphic novel. She lives in Queens, New York, and you can visit her online at kellyfernandez.net.